I0621894

PENRYN EDITIONS

GATHERED PIECES

"The author's detailed descriptions of the physical environment in these pieces contrasts with her sparse descriptions of the characters, who she paints with light strokes.

This contrast is magical, drawing us deeply into the psyche of the characters and their world.

Often the characters are merely suggested by small gestures or off-handed remarks, and the reader's observation of these produces genuine sympathy instead of cold, intellectual understanding."

Karl Kaiser, an astute reader

GATHERED PIECES

A collection of narratives by

Mitchell Hagerstrom

Penryn Editions 2019

GATHERED PIECES

Copyright © 2019 by Mitchell Hagerstrom

Published by

PENRYN EDITIONS

Penryn Editions P.O. Box 167
Queenstown, Maryland 21658

ISBN : 978-1-7330086-4-8

The author would like to thank The Open End and The Pacific Review where some of these pieces appeared, often in much different versions.

Cover photo by Mitchell Hagerstrom.

AUTHOR'S NOTE

My characters are thieves. I've encouraged such thievery by leaving windows open and doors unlocked.

I've allowed them access to the places I've lived, down to the very beds I've slept in.

They have helped themselves to food off my tables, and words from the mouths of friends, relatives, even strangers I've eavesdropped upon.

These pieces were created from tales I'd been told, from scenes I'd glimpsed merely from the corner of an eye, from my own memories, but most are a mix of all these sources.

The collection comprises both early and more recent work, gathered together, and polished as best I can.

Mitchell Hagerstrom
Austin, Texas

"I am quite alone. I am neither happy nor unhappy. I lie suspended like a hair or a feather in the cloudy mixtures of memory."

-- Lawrence Durrell

CONTENTS

SOUTHERN CALIFORNIA

AN AFTERNOON AT THE AMBASSADOR   3
ORNAMENTAL BRUISES   5
THE RUNAWAYS   11
GREY IS THE COLOR   15
FREDDY LAMARR   17
WHAT DO YOU DREAM ?   23
A PILLOW   27

MISSOURI

FOLLOW DIRECTIONS   33
ETHAN, ETHAN   39
FLORENCE   45

SAN FRANCISCO

WILD HORSES   57
XMAS TREES   59
WORKING GIRL   65
SLUMMING   67
LUNCH WITH FRANCIS   69

MEXICO

THE TOURIST   77

EL GUAPO   93

LOUISIANA

ICE STORM, MANSFIELD   97

MY FATHER'S WATCH   99

SOUTHERN
CALIFORNIA

AN AFTERNOON AT THE AMBASSADOR

On a private tour we're shown through
A shiny kitchen, then down a dingy hallway
To a wide pantry. There's no plaque,
No reminder that Robert Kennedy bled out
On that dirty floor. Assassinated.

Subdued, we retreat to the hotel's bistro,
Order icy martinis and a tray of briny oysters.
A squeeze of lemon, then a bite to release
That coppery metallic taste, and they slide
Down our throats, like soft bullets.

***

ORNAMENTAL BRUISES

At a small table beneath an open window, two women sit talking while drinking from tall cans and filling an ashtray. It's a quiet neighborhood where everyone is either watching late night TV. or in bed with a book or a lover. There's the drone of crickets, like a radio turned low to play all night long.

"Tired?" Gina asks. "You want for me to go home?"

Linda shakes her head, then lifts her arms and runs her fingers through her hair. She croons, "summer-time an' the liv'n ain't eeeeee-zzzz."

"IS easy," Gina says, "not ain't."

"But it ain't," Linda says.

Gina shrugs.

"We ought to go somewhere," Linda says, "get something to eat. Go splash your face, and I'll get you something else to wear."

When Gina stands, she knocks against the table, nearly upsetting a water-glass of full-blown white roses. One of the blossoms shatters, and as Linda watches they all shatter one by one. The sound of the petals hitting the table is sub-audible.

After her husband had scrunched down in the tub, fully dressed, still wearing his shoes, and slit his own throat, Linda had moved. Now, standing in the doorway of this bathroom, she holds out a blouse dotted with blue cornflowers.

Gina removes her T-shirt, which was torn at one shoulder, and washes her face and neck. She finishes patting herself dry, then turns and holds the towel to her breast.

"What the hell!" Linda says. "You told me he didn't hit you."

"He didn't," Gina says. "He only shook me."

"But your arms are covered in bruises," Linda says. "I'll get you something long-sleeved."

"It's okay," Gina says, reaching for the blouse. "Besides, this is pretty."

The coffee shop at a nearby motel is dark, but the

bar is open. The women settle on stools, facing a display of bottles and their own reflections in the large mirror. The bartender straightens up from where he was hunched over talking to his only customer at the other end of the bar.

Linda orders a couple of vodka Collins and pushes a basket of pretzels toward her friend. "Here," she says.

Gina eats a pretzel, and before their drinks come, she eats several more.

"Didn't know it was so late," Linda says. "One drink then we'll go find something to eat."

"Any more cigarettes?" Gina asks.

Linda hands her the pack, first taking one for herself. She then pulls her sunglasses from her purse and puts them on. "I wish I had one of those fancy cigarette holders," she says, staring at herself in the huge mirror.

Gina takes out her sunglasses and puts them on.

"Why do you take it?" Linda asks her friend's reflection in the mirror.

Gina answers: "I figured you of all people might understand."

Linda sighs. "You're a fool," she says. "Kirk never hit me, never gave me bruises."

Linda's Kirk had been a medic. His nightmares were never violent, but he did have them. After a while, he gave up sleeping. Instead, he taught himself to whittle, trying for the skill of a couple of his elderly cousins. They were so good that they made chains, long strands of connected links from only one piece of wood. Many nights, Kirk whittled until daylight.

"Jimmy doesn't have nightmares very often," Gina says. "And then, all he ever does is grab my arms and shake. He thinks he's still in Nam, driving a truck down a pot-holed road through a jungle with spook snipers behind every tree. Can't tell you how many times he drove through attempted ambushes, bullets flying everywhere."

"He's certifiable," Linda says. "They all are. That's what the war did, what it took from them, that's what it took from me and you. Is he still taking his meds?"

"He doesn't like them," Gina answers. "He says they don't help at all.

"Gotta say they didn't help Kirk," Linda adds. "Oh, they made him calm, but in the end, they didn't save him."

The bar stays as empty as when they came in, only the bartender talking to the man at the far end. Just before closing, Linda orders two more drinks and a six-pack to go. Both women, eyes hidden behind sunglasses, lean against the bar's padded cushion and stare at themselves in the mirror behind the row of liquor bottles.

"Doesn't this place ever close?" Gina asks.

Linda looks down to where the bartender is still talking to the man at the other end. "He doesn't seem to be in any hurry to kick us out," she says. "Here, have a beer." She pushes the six-pack toward Gina.

Linda trips on the last step and Gina slips an arm under her elbow and lifts. The two women lean into each other as though into a strong wind. Linda fumbles with her keys. Inside, she turns on a small lamp.

"How 'bout some music," she says. "You 'member how to work that old turntable?"

"Yeah," Gina says, slumping into a chair. "Whaddya want?"

"Anything," Linda answers from the kitchen, as she puts the two remaining beers in the refrigerator.

Gina slides to the floor, crawls over and puts on the first record she lays her hands on. The music starts with a muted trumpet accompanied by a lazy, one-handed piano.

Linda comes to the doorway, says, "it's been a long time since I heard that."

"It wasn't put away," Gina says.

A legendary chanteuse begins the lyrics of an old-fashioned ballad.

The phrasing is hesitant, and her voice no longer pure.

Hands on hips, Linda crosses the room clumsily. Gina stands and holds open her arms.

Holding each other lightly, the women dance, turning in slow, awkward circles. While they dance a greyish, pre-dawn light comes through the open windows. In the eaves some small birds begin to sing.

When the song ends, resting in the empty groove before the next one, Linda puts her head on Gina's shoulder and, without saying a word, begins to cry.

Gina holds her friend tighter. She knows that if she were drowning, Linda would swim down to rescue her, would press her mouth to hers, and open it to share what meager air she had, even if it meant she could not save herself.

***

THE RUNAWAYS

The place was borrowed from a friend of a friend, a rustic cabin perched on the side of a narrow mountain canyon. In the kitchen a potted plant, dying from too much water, had been pushed to one side of the round table that had only two chairs. From outside came the yellow air of an unspectacular sunset, and the sounds of an occasional car or truck downshifting for the sharp turn in front of the place.

The woman and the girl sat in the two chairs and opened bags of fast food which they laid out on paper napkins. The girl took very deliberate bites which raised her upper lip, exposing a row of braces. She reached out and touched the shingled wall. "Did he do this?" she asked.

"Probably," the woman said.

"Look at all those bottles," the girl said.

The woman twisted in her chair to see a hutch displaying assorted bottles of beer, odd domestic ones and even odder foreign ones.

"Did he drink all those?" the girl asked.

The woman shook her head. "No, he drinks near beer," she said.

"Near beer, what's that?"

"Pretend beer."

"Why?"

The woman smiled. "He's silly."

With the last of her hamburger in one hand, the girl went over to the hutch and picked up a bottle.

"What's ale?" she asked.

The woman told the girl to put it down because her hands were greasy.

"This hand isn't greasy," the girl said, but she put the bottle back and did not pick up another.

Again, she asked: "What's ale?"

"Just another kind of beer," the woman said. She had finished her French fries and reached for the girl's.

"You can have them all," the girl said, pushing

them away. "I'm full."

Instead, the woman gathered everything together and stuffed it back in the bags.

"I'm gonna have a club soda," she said, "you want anything?"

The girl shook her head and went to stand in the doorway to the other room. "Why does he have a stuffed raccoon?" she asked.

"Who knows," the woman said. She was at the sink, struggling with an old-fashioned ice tray.

"I don't like it," the girl said, "and I don't like the snakeskin on the wall, and I don't like the skull with the Jewish hat."

The woman sighed. "We can put that away," she said.

"You do it," the girl said. "I'm not touching it."

They both went into the other room and the woman set her glass on the mantle.

"It's not a Jewish hat," she said. "Persian, maybe. Or Peruvian?"

The front room was dim and the canyon traffic louder. Headlights had begun to rake the windows, seeping through gaps in the Venetians.

The girl sat down on the edge of the sofa. "Is it real?" she asked.

The woman picked up the skull. "Probably plastic," she said, as she crossed the room to the closet where she placed it on a high shelf behind some Christmas stuff. She then turned to the girl and held out her arms.

"Well," she said, "you wanna dance?"

The girl gave a snort of laughter, scooted farther back on the sofa, and asked: "You gonna sleep with me tonight?"

***

GREY IS THE COLOR

Of foggy morning dawns, days without sunsets,

Rainy afternoons and empty wine bottles.

The legendary color of Guinevere's eyes, that grey,

And the clichés of smoke, slate, doves, battleships.

It's the hopelessness of a phone

Ringing in an empty house,

Or of a locked trunk with no key,

Or dreams that can't be remembered.

It's Venice in November.

It's a couple on a dark street corner

In a whispered argument and one walks away

Without looking back.

***

FREDDY LAMARR

Mac turns off the ignition, lifts his foot from the clutch, and pulls up the emergency brake. The car's aircon is fucked up, and for the whole drive his open windows drenched him with barely breathable, super-heated, humid air. He pushes his heat wilted hair from a sweaty forehead and looks up at the familiar building, a brutally massive structure. But that's how jails are designed these days.

He leaves the car unlocked and the windows down, figuring no one would be fool enough to mess with it in this parking lot. Inside, he paces the small meeting room for attorneys and their clients. He wishes it were larger, wishes for a corner to fart in: instead he sits in one of the two chairs. What with clangings of metal against metal, of barred doors opening and shutting, the room always feels like it's vibrating.

A porky face with no neck, perched on a uniformed torso, leans in the door. "James MacNamara?"

Mac nods.

"Frederick Lamarr Brown? Freddy Brown, right?"

"That's right," Mac says.

The porky face leaves and a slim, strikingly handsome black man slides through the doorway. Two steps, two long-legged Nureyev-like glides, and he is at the table.

"Hey, Freddy," Mac says, half rising from his chair, and awkwardly taking the offered hand, a hand poised as though to be kissed, not shaken.

Seated now in the chair opposite, Freddy smiles. "What's up?"

Mac carefully lifts his still sweaty trousers from his thighs and sits. "Got the police report," he says, opening a file on the table and fumbling with papers.

"I didn't talk," Freddy says. "Just like you told me last time. I didn't talk."

"No, you didn't give a statement this time, but your john was wired."

Freddy squirms. "But I told him for free. Ain't no crime if'en for free."

"Yeah," Mac nods. "But, Freddy, you started at twenty bucks. Came down to ten, then five. Christ. Then for free. You didn't start off for free."

"Girl's gotta make a livin'," Freddy says with a pout.

Mac frowns sympathetically. "Sorry, pal, they got you cold. I told you, the john was wearing a wire."

Freddy shrugs. "This here jail's not bad, for a while. But these here," he strokes the front of his jail-issue jumpsuit. "These here ain't my idea of lookin' good. And there ain't too many pretty boys in here this time. All them ugly old dudes trying to put the make on me. And here, ya know, ya can't pick and choose. Don't want my pretty face smashed, ya know."

Mac interrupts, "You gonna bail?"

Freddy lifts his hands, poor-like, and repeats, "Not that bad in here."

"Just as well," Mac says. "At sentencing, I can probably get you out for time served. That's if you behave yourself." He's relieved that Freddy isn't bailing. Better for him to show up in court in jail-issue rather than 5-inch heels and his working clothes. Freddy dressed for the streets is more than most judges can handle. "I'm sure the D.A. will deal. Cops don't wanna waste a good snitch, putting him on the stand. Out in public, you know."

"Okay, then," Freddy says, and stands to leave while Mac gathers his papers. Freddy knocks at the small window in the door to alert the guard, then turns back. "He was a real pretty one," he sighs. "I shoulda started for free."

A month after Freddy's release and he's back. The guy at the Defender's Office who makes assignments can't help himself, always gives Freddy to Mac. Anyway, still summertime, but at least the aircon in the car's been fixed.

"You know, Freddy," Mac says when they're seated, "I'm getting some awful teasing at the office. Them saying me and you are an item."

Freddy screams with laughter, then quickly clamps one slim elegant-fingered hand over his mouth. "Mac, honey," he says, "you ain't my type. Not 'nless you got some real foldin' money."

They both laugh.

"Okay, now," Mac says. "Straighten up. I need you to listen. This time we are going to trial."

Freddy's eyebrows go up. "But, but ...."

Mac says, "Shhh, listen. We're gonna get a dismissal. We're gonna ask for a judge, not a jury. Been looking at the calendar and I'm pretty sure we won't be assigned some asshole judge. Entrapment is what it is. All a judge gotta do is look at the law. They offered you candy. Right?"

Freddy nods. "I knew it was a cop. He come on to me and I said, nope. When he said how about for a Tootsie Roll, I figured he was joking. Sure, I said. Then he comes back with a whole bag of candy. I don't even like Tootsie Rolls. They look like poodle doo-doo. But he was gettin'pushy, shoving that bag of candy at me. So, I took it. Soon as I had hold of it, he said, you're busted. And that was that."

Mac shakes his head. "What a dumb shit. Not you, Freddy. Dumb shit cop."

Freddy giggles. "You gonna get me off?" he asks.

"Don't bail," Mac tells him. "We don't wanna press our luck, even if we get Hamilton." The judge he names is the least hard-assed on the bench.

The day in court goes down just as Mac said it would. On the stand the cop makes an utter fool of himself, with the judge leaning over, and saying, "Tootsie Rolls? You got to be kidding me," and the cop's face getting redder and redder.

The judge turns to Mac: "Counselor?"

Mac, with a big smirk on his face, says, "Defense calls for motion for dismissal of charges."

The judge bangs the hammer: "Motion granted; case dismissed!"

Freddy and Mac shake hands as the cop weasels himself out the back door. The prosecutor comes over and gives Mac a pat on the shoulder. Mac turns to him. "The problem in this town isn't street vice," Mac says. The prosecutor nods, "I know," he answers.

"Yeah," Freddy whispers to Mac, in a stage whisper, "and a girl's gotta make a livin'." Everyone within ten feet, including the prosecutor, gets the giggles.

***

WHAT DO YOU DREAM?

The woman found him relaxing in the deep, old-fashioned tub, his eyes closed and water up to his chin, kneecaps like islands.

"Hey," she said, from the doorway.

The man opened his eyes and sat up.

The woman displayed a wine bottle and two glasses. He shook his head; said he didn't want any.

"It's a nice cheery red," she said, coming into the room and sitting down on the floor. She poured two glasses and handed him one. He took it, tipped it toward her in a toast, and told her she looked nice. She smiled and tipped her glass to him.

Scooting back to lean against the wall, she spilled some wine on the cradle of her skirt. She watched as it bled into the white cotton. Not a small spill, the stain grew and grew.

"You'd better rinse that out," he said.

"Too late on this fabric," she replied. "It's a goner."

She traced the stain with her fingers. "Reminds me of my first time," she said. "I remember being very nervous. It's a bit like a flower, isn't it? Maybe I should spill a bit more here and here," she said, dipping her fingers in her glass and flicking wine drops across her skirt. "I can embroider around all the stains. Just imagine a cluster of old roses."

The man said nothing. He finished off his wine and shook his head when she offered more.

"There's a convent church in Spain," she said. "I forget exactly where and I forget the name, but it has large pieces of linen under glass, in big gilt frames. They're the stained sheets from the wedding nights of local noblewomen."

The man snorted. "Wherever did you hear that!"

"Who knows," she said, struggling to her feet. She moved to the small window that looked out over a field of summer-spent grass and wild sunflowers. Placing her glass on the windowsill, she turned, and dropped to her knees behind him. She touched the back of his head, his neck, and whispered in his ear: "Maybe I dreamt it."

The man snorted at that, too.

Her hand traced the curve of his shoulder and slid down into the water.

"It's cold," she said.

"It's okay," he answered.

The woman reached the length of his arm and took away the empty glass. She stood and placed it beside hers on the windowsill. Twilight was beginning to put a purple edge on the straw-colored field, and the small golden sunflowers nodded their heads in a tiny breeze.

She came back and knelt beside the tub. She put her hands on the rim, her chin on her hands, and looked at him.

"Tell me," she said. "What do you dream?"

***

A PILLOW

He brushed my hand away from his ear where I had been tracing its shape with a fingernail.

"You sleepy?" I asked.

He gave a small sigh.

I turned over onto my back and pulled up the sheet. "Did I ever tell you what my sister said?" I asked.

"Which one?"

"Laurie."

No response, so I continued: "Laurie told me my mother said my father was a great lover and Laurie asked her how she knew, like who did she compare him with? My mother told her she didn't have to compare, she just knew."

"You mean, your mother never fucked anyone else?"

I shrugged.

"So," he said. "Do you compare?"

I turned to him and whispered: "you're in-com-parable."

He rolled over, away from me.

"My mother once told me about when she was being treated for some female infection and my father had to wear a condom. She said she liked not having to sleep on the wet spot."

"What're you saying?"

"Nothing. I'm just telling you about my mother."

"You saying you always get the wet spot?"

"No. I'm not saying that at all."

He turned on his side again, away from me.

"Don't do that," I said, and I spooned myself along his length, wrapped my arm around him and placed my hand over his heart. I told him: "I remember once when my father had a trip back East and after he left, I found my mother crying. She told me she was crying because she hadn't slept with my father before he left. She said they'd had a silly argument."

"My parents fought all the time," he said.

"I know."

"Tell me something else," he said, "something not about your mother."

I put my forehead against his back and thought for a moment. "In *Mah Jong*," I said," that game? Did you know a pair of tiles is called a pillow?"

He pulled my arm around him tighter. "You on the wet spot?" he asked.

***

MISSOURI

FOLLOWING DIRECTIONS

Between them they carry small tools and the parts to the new barbecue. They cross the lawn and settle in the shade of the maple. From there, the man can hear the conversation between his new wife and their friend Victor up on the patio.

"Okay," the man's stepdaughter says, to get his attention. She tosses her braids back over her shoulders, and begins to read aloud from the instruction sheet: "Connect the leg pieces to the underside of the main unit at points A, B & C using brackets D, E, & F." Then, one by one, she hands him the legs.

"I know what you mean," the man hears his wife say, and he looks over, sees their friend Victor shake his head and his wife put her hand over her eyes.

"B to E," his stepdaughter says, and the man turns back to securing the legs to the main unit.

"So," he says to her, "what do you think of Victor?"

"Victor?"

"Yeah, Victor. You think he's good looking?"

She looks over at her mother and Victor. "I guess so," she says, but with an exaggerated shrug.

When the legs are connected, the man says, "what's next?"

She hands him the wheels. But first you put that there, she says, then you attach the wheels.

The man hears his wife laugh. "My mother was just like that," he hears her say. And when he looks over, she's pantomiming a gesture he has never seen before.

The man points the screwdriver toward the patio. "Ever see your mother or your grandmother do that?" he asks.

"Do what?"

The man sets the tool down and mimics his wife's gesture. His stepdaughter laughs and shakes her head.

The man slips a brace between the legs of the barbecue, tightens it, and then begins to add, one by one, the wheels.

"Such a crazy night," he hears his wife say, "did I catch hell!" Victor is laughing.

The man frowns. "Does your mother ever tell you stories about when she was young? You know, from when she was a girl."

"I guess. Sometimes."

"Like what? What does she say?"

"I donno know. I don't remember."

The man looks over at the patio. He watches as his wife lifts her hair off her neck, holds it for a while on the top of her head, and then lets it fall.

"The first thing I remember?" he hears her say.

The man stops working and listens. She's never told him the first thing she remembers.

"I must've been four," she says, "and my parents were getting ready to go out. My mother prancing around and fixing her face in the vanity. I picked up her pearls and put them on, but my little brother grabbed them and when I pulled, he pulled, and they broke. Scattered all over the floor. Before I knew it, my father had lifted me up by one arm, squeezing so hard I thought he had broken it. Years later I learned the pearls had been his wedding present to her."

"Why did she tell him that?" the man asks. "She never told me about that."

"It's all finished," his stepdaughter says in a soft voice.

Just then Victor stands and goes into the house. His wife calls over: "You ready for a drink?"

The man shakes his head and turns to his stepdaughter. At the wedding she had stood beside her mother and both of them had worn mock orange blossoms in their hair. He remembers hoping he would be a good father.

He hands her the screwdriver. "Could you put the tools away for me, ... love?"

Then he walks over to the patio. His wife meets him at the edge of the bricks. "Sure, you don't wanna a drink?" she asks, putting her hands on his shoulders.

He looks at the fine bones in her face, lets his fingers trace her fragile clavicle. He starts to reach for her hands, but lets his arms drop instead.

"What?" she says, sliding her hands down his arms and putting her forehead against his. He puts his arms around her just as Victor comes out with their fresh drinks.

"Hey, you two," Victor calls, "the honeymoon's over." The man looks over at his friend and forces a smile.

"Come," his wife says, stepping down off the patio. "Come, show me what you two did."

Together they walk toward the maple tree. His wife takes one of his arms and wraps it around her shoulder, then wraps one of hers around his waist. As they walk, he looks down at her feet, bare on the freshly mowed grass, and he caresses her arm. Lightly.

***

ETHAN, ETHAN

The man moved the rocking chair to in front of the large window in the dining room. From there he could look down, a story below, to the patio where birds flocked around the feeder and then across into a vast canopy of trees. Beyond was wilderness, and the leaves were already turning.

The ringing of the wall phone startled him. The man half stood to lift the receiver, but before putting it to his ear he sat back down.

"Hello," he said in a quiet, inquiring voice.

"Hey! How come you haven't called me?" It was his brother in another city in another time zone.

"I've been busy. I've had my mind on other things," the man said.

"Soooo, how's it going," his brother asked. "You know, how's the weather?"

"Fine," the man said. "I'm looking out the back window and the weather looks just fine."

"That's not what I meant," his brother replied. "I meant, how're you feeling? How's Mary Ellen and the baby? You know."

"Everyone's fine," the man said.

"I had been waiting for your call. You said you'd call."

"I know," the man said, "but like I said, I've been real busy. Matter of fact, I'm real busy right now. I've got Ethan and he's being fussy. How about I call you back?" As the man said this, he curved one arm to rest on the arm of the rocker as if he were really holding a baby.

"Put him on," his brother said. I wanna talk to him."

"Not now, Frankie," the man said.

"Oh, come on. Lemme talk to him."

"Okay, okay," the man said, talk to him, and he held the receiver out in the air for a while before putting it back to his ear. He could hear his brother: "Hey, Ethan, Ethan! It's your Uncle Frank. Say hi to your Uncle Frank." Then: "Hey, Marty, he yelled, what's he doing? Is he listening?"

"Yeah," the man said, "he's listening."

"So how come he doesn't say something?"

"You know, Frankie, he's not old enough to talk."

"Okay, then pinch him. Make him make a noise."

"I'm not gonna pinch my own kid."

"Come on, just a little one. I wanna hear him make a noise."

"Listen, Frankie, I'm busy. I'll call you back."

"Hold on, Marty. I just called with the blue."

"Okay, what is it? Ten?"

"The blue says ten. Remember what you paid? Wasn't it fifteen?"

"Yeah, maybe fifteen. I don't remember."

"So, ask Mary Ellen."

"She's not here right now."

"Well, fuck, when she gets home for christsakes. What's the matter with you!"

"Nothing. There's nothing the matter with me. Anyway, we decided we don't wanna sell the car. Mary Ellen doesn't wanna sell the car."

"She still giving you a bad time, huh?"

The man stood up. "She's not giving me a bad time, Frankie, so just drop it." The man pressed his forehead against the windowpane. It was icy cold, but the sun was bright outside. He was surprised at how cold the glass was.

"Damn, Marty," his brother said. "I thought you two had things worked out."

"Just drop it," the man said, moving toward the kitchen. He was trying to make the phone cord reach the liquor cabinet.

"You know", his brother said, "Gloria locks herself in the bathroom once in a while, but you can talk through a bathroom door."

"Frankie, the baby fell asleep. I gotta go put him down. I'll call you back later."

"I'll wait," his brother said. "Go put him down."

The man let the receiver dangle along the wall while he went into the kitchen. There he poured himself a big slog of scotch, not bothering with ice or water, and carried it back to the rocker. He set the drink on the windowsill. When he sat back, he noted that the dogwood leaves were beginning to show red along the edges and the birds were in a flurry around the feeder.

"Hey," his brother yelled.

The man leaned forward, elbows on knees, intent on the outside action.

"Hey, you still there?" his brother yelled.

The man stood and cradled the receiver. He returned to the rocker to wait for his brother to call back, a call he had no intention of answering.

Outside the birds were still in a flurry around the feeder and the dogwood still turning. And his drink was as yet untouched.

**

FLORENCE

When Muriel called with an invitation to join them for dinner, Harry nearly dropped the phone. Muriel's husband, John, had been the lover of Harry's former wife. Was there such a thing as a statute of limitations for holding grudges against a colleague for fucking one's wife? Harry had never heard of such and was so dumbfounded by the gall of Muriel's invitation, he accepted.

When Harry discovered his wife and John were having an affair, he told himself it was just a fling. Everyone knew John had a reputation as a ladies' man. Harry found himself unable to confront his wife and while he dithered, she packed and left. Her note gave no reason, just that she was gone and would not return. Harry had no idea how or why the affair with John ended. Their lawyers took care of everything and Harry had not seen his wife since.

Although Harry and John taught at the same university, the pair were able to avoid each other. Their offices were on different floors of a large building. On those rare occasions when they had to attend the same meeting, they were quite agile at not making eye contact and pretending to be busy consulting some important paperwork.

Still, between Harry's acceptance of Muriel's invitation and the actual event, he tried to find a plausible way to bow out. Daily he mulled over his options. He even went to the college library to consult the Emily Post etiquette books, but found no answer, no polite way of backing out.

Then, a few days before the event, Muriel left a message with his secretary asking, if he wouldn't mind, could he bring pictures of his sabbatical because she and John were also considering Italy for John's sabbatical. Harry truly regretted not hanging up on the woman when she first called.

On the designated evening he took care with his grooming and his dress, then stuffed his pockets with photos from his sabbatical year, mostly Polaroids. Still, even as he knocked on the door, he puzzled over Muriel's motive for the invitation. Perhaps she had not known about his wife and John?

Harry and his wife had been guests at this house, not for intimate dinners, but had been included in the large groups of faculty when John and Muriel hosted buffets and cocktail parties. The place looked much as he remembered. After handshakes and chucking the baby under the chin, Harry was introduced to a fellow guest, a young woman who, he learned, was one of Muriel's grad students.

During drinks before dinner Harry brought out his photos. John shuffled through them, rarely pausing, sometimes frowning. Muriel looked over John's shoulder while bouncing the baby on her knees. The pictures were then passed to the young woman who lingered over no one picture more than another and made no comments except to admire the light in certain of them where the light was extraordinary.

Harry thought it odd that no one, not John or Muriel or the young woman, commented on the images of the woman, Harry's wife, who was so prominent in the photos: a head-shot at the foot of

David's famous feet, or holding onto her hat as she craned back to gaze up at a church facade, or presenting her lovely posterior to the camera as she bent over a balustrade to peer down at the dirty river.

Then, as proper at a dinner parties, they chatted about Italy in general, since that seemed to be the purpose of the gathering. The baby who was a little less than a year at the time, started kicking up a fuss. The young woman held out her arms and took him. She stood him on her lap, but he threw himself against her, circled her neck with his arms, opened his mouth wide and placed it on hers. When he leaned back, he was laughing and holding on to her hair, a handful in each fist. Harry was mesmerized by the scene and realized that in sunlight the young woman's hair would be the same deep-golden shade as his former wife's.

John had made *osso buco* with a creamy polenta, and everything was superb. They dined at a small, informal table near the kitchen. The dinner conversation followed the usual: campus gossip, the weather, and some of the newer books and films. During this, Harry learned that John and Muriel often engaged the young woman as a babysitter, especially when they had to be away for weekend conferences.

After dinner, when Muriel had taken the baby upstairs and the young woman had gone to powder her nose, Harry watched as John exchanged wine glasses, his empty for the young woman's which was still half full. When she returned, she reached across for her wine glass, took a sip, and set it back down in front of John.

That was all, just the familiarity or intimacy of them drinking from the same glass. And then, the young woman turned to Harry. "Tell us more about Florence," she said.

Harry cleared his throat and began to remove his wife from those photographs, as though scraping away her bright image with a knife point or a razor blade. "How misleading the soft light in those pictures," he said, "how cold the fogs coming off that murky, muddy river, how damp and comfortless those Italian houses." He made the place sound miserable. He didn't know why. That year in Florence had been the highlight of his marriage.

When Muriel returned from putting the baby to bed, the young woman excused herself to help with the clean-up. Harry watched as Muriel handed the young woman the dishes one by one after they were rinsed. He noted that when the young woman filled the lower rack of the dishwasher, she bent from the hips, keeping her back and legs straight, her knees locked, as though performing some kind of dance exercise, not a household chore. But there had been no mention that she was a dancer.

Harry's wife had been a dancer in her younger days. He remembered one of their first outings together, a rather stuffy lecture on ecclesiastic architecture. She had worn a red dress, more suitable for a different kind of evening.

The dishwasher filled, Muriel served coffee and fancy chocolates, and then the evening was over. As Harry was thanking Muriel and gathering his things, John and the young woman stepped out on the dark porch. Harry heard John say: "Goodnight." And then, after a pause, a pause Harry thought long enough for a kiss, he heard John say, "sleep well."

A month or so later, Harry left for Newfoundland, to the same small fishing village where he had been spending his summers, a wonderfully quiet place to write, and finish projects, and to escape from the latest gossip and colleagues wanting to share it.

On his return home, Harry learned that John

and Muriel were not going to Florence in the fall as planned. Instead, they were staying in town and it was rumored they were separated and were probably divorcing.

Just before classes started in the fall, Harry found himself one night bored and needing distraction. He took himself across the river, to a rundown place with pool tables, a place that played melancholic country songs instead of the loud thumping kind of music that attracts students. He should have remembered John also knew of the place. There they were.

She was leaning over a pool table, her hold on the cue stick a bit uncertain, awkward even. Harry watched. She shook her hair back over her shoulders and looked across to John who had placed a finger lightly on the opposite rim of the table. She moved her eyes back to the ball. Her stroke was sure, and the designated target rolled into a pocket.

Again, and again she followed John's directions until she had run the table and there was a shout of laughter from them both. And then, John turned to Harry, who thought he had not been noticed, and said: "Together we play better than I do alone."

The young woman laughed. "But I can't cook,"

she said.

"That's true, she can't," John confirmed.

Harry shrugged. "No matter," he said.

John invited him to join them. Beers were ordered and they settled around one of the small tables.

John asked what Harry had been up to, and so he told them about his summer, about his nearly finished project, but not about his fears that it would never be published.

When he realized they weren't listening or interested, he made an intentional change of subject, and declared: "Florence is lovely." And then added, with a bit of spite, "I heard you're not going."

"I'm not," John said, and the young woman looked down and began picking at the label on her beer bottle, her hair falling across her face. John reached over and tucked it behind her ear. Before anything else was said, the young woman stood, shouldered her purse and left the table, heading toward the hallway to the ladies'.

John turned to watch her. John said, "I'm sure you heard."

Harry nodded.

"Muriel is being great about it, although she

plagues me with increasing demands: taking the boy for haircuts, making sure he's given ear medicine when he's with me, and constantly changing the pickup times for my custody days."

When the young woman reappeared in the entrance to the hallway, John abruptly ended our conversation. The young woman was not alone, a townie was with her and they were chuckling over something.

John pushed back from the table and moved quickly across the room. Harry heard John bark at the unknown townie who slithered away. John then grabbed the young woman's arm and pulled her back into the shadowed hallway. She shoved him with surprising strength and no sign of fear. But, when she turned from him, he grabbed her arm again, then took her by the throat and began shaking her. Harry heard a strangled cry. And then John's mouth covered hers and his hands moved from her throat, down to pull her tightly against him. Soft kisses, tears and whispers. John held her a minute longer, then pushed open the back door and they were gone.

Harry left his unfinished beer and went up to the bar. He ordered something stronger, something he could put to his lips as a substitute for love, a substitute for passion if he drank enough of them. And before taking himself three sheets or even ten sheets to the wind, he wondered if John had ever noted the irony of Florence being his wife's name, and if John had ever noticed that his new young woman and Florence had that same dark golden shade of hair.

***

SAN
FRANCISCO

WILD HORSES
for Laura (1957-1986)

An overcast sky, an empty beach, and an ocean that's not its usual pacific self. Imagine, if you will, a stormy sea in an antique sepia-toned lithograph. Imagine towering waves with wind-whipped crests lifting high into the air, mimicking the flowing manes of mythical horses.

Behind us on the seawall someone had painted a string of sturdy, over-sized horses. They reminded me of those robust women Picasso painted as they frolicked on the beach at Cannes, and of those prehistoric horse drawings in French and Spanish caves. But most of all, I was reminded that horse is slang for heroin.

When my mother opened the box, the wind caught and lifted my sister's ashes, smeared them across my mother's tear-dampened face. My father reached out to help but she swatted his hands away. Gently, he took the box from her, gathered her into his arms, and passed the box to my brother who put his back to the wind and flicked his wrist: once, twice, three times, and our blue-eyed girl was gone.

***

XMAS TREES

On a night in mid-December, the woman passed a Xmas tree lot on a corner where an old three-story Victorian had been torn down in the spring. The lot was lit by a string of lights propped on tall, precarious poles. When she stepped into the dense stand of trees, it was like being in the middle of a real forest. She wandered about, studying the trees and admiring certain ones.

A broad-shouldered man in a tartan flannel shirt, a man who looked like he himself had chopped down the trees, came over and asked if he could help.

She pointed to a tree she liked. "What kind is that?" she asked.

"They're called Silver Tip", he told her, "but

they're actually red firs. They last better than the Douglas. Sturdier because they grow at higher elevations."

"Thank you," she said. "I was just looking."

Later that night, during a program she and her husband usually watched, she waited for a commercial, then turned to him and asked if he'd seen the Xmas tree lot.

"What lot?"

"On the corner of Webster."

He shook his head.

She moved closer to him on the sofa. "I think we should have a tree this year," she said.

He said nothing and then the program came back on.

"So," she said, "could we have a tree?"

"Shh," he said, "I can't hear."

The trees began falling a few days after Xmas. Walking home one morning from the corner bakery, the woman saw her first one. It caught her eye as it dropped past the second story of the building across the street. Bottom heavy, it landed on its base with a smack and then toppled over onto its side. Strands of tinsel still clung to some of the branches.

After hanging her coat in the hall, she called out to her husband: "I just saw a Xmas tree commit suicide."

She could see him hunched over his desk under the front windows.

She went into the kitchen. "The rolls are still warm," she called.

He pushed back his chair. She watched through the doorway as he stood staring out the window for a minute. When he came into the kitchen he asked if the rolls were still warm.

"They are," she said, then added, "I wish we'd had a tree this year."

"Christ," he said, "would you lay off it."

The next day, the woman spent several hours watching the six-story apartment building across the street. She saw three trees fall, one from beginning to end. A window on the fourth floor opened and the head of an elderly woman leaned out and looked down. Then, the elderly head drew back inside, and the head of a tree appeared.

Quickly, the whole tree was out the window. It hung in mid-air for a millisecond and then dropped, twisting to an upright position before hitting the pavement.

The following morning, as soon as her husband left for work, the woman began making cookies. She rolled the dough very thin and cut rounds with a water glass. With a knife point, she tried her best to carve angels in the dough. She could not get the wings quite right but sprinkled them with sugar and put them in the oven to bake. Then, while they were still hot, she made holes in them for hanging.

When she thought her husband would be back from lunch, she called him. He was a deputy D.A. assigned to Family Law.

"What are you doing?" she asked.

"The usual," he said, "non-support."

"Are you working late?" she asked.

"Not tonight," he said. "What's for dinner?"

She told him she hadn't decided. When she hung up, she left the building and circled her block several times before she found the right one. In the elevator, a neighbor she didn't know rode up with her and her Xmas tree. She figured he was giving her funny looks, but she ignored him and kept her eyes on the floor.

The tree's wooden foot brace was still intact, and she set the tree in the corner. Then, she took a box of paper clips from the desk, spilled some out and bent them open. A number of the cookies crumbled, but most held. When she finished, she wished she had a star for the top.

She fixed herself a cup of hot chocolate, adding a splash of brandy. Sitting on the sofa, she cupped her hands around the hot mug and hummed to herself. She tried singing carols, but found she couldn't remember enough words, couldn't remember any one song all the way through.

She had some more brandy and hot chocolate, but still could not remember the songs of her childhood Xmases. When it got close to the time her husband would be home, she opened the window and threw the tree out, cookies and all. She was just putting the vacuum away when her husband called saying he would be a bit late and he'd bring Chinese.

"Fine," she said, "that's just fine."

After trying harder, but unsuccessfully, to remember those damned songs, and pouring herself several more brandies, she found herself reaching across the desk and opening the window.

Both the sky and the building across the street were dark. A soft rain was falling. She shivered a little, rubbed her arms, and then began opening desk drawers and pulling out the contents, tossing everything out the window – pens, pencils, note pads, envelopes, bills, all her husband's papers and all her own papers.

"What the hell!" she heard her husband's voice behind her. He came and leaned out the window beside her.

A few of the papers were still floating down and someone on the sidewalk was staring up from under his or her umbrella. It was impossible to tell if it was a man or a woman.

"What the hell!" her husband repeated.

The wet street and sidewalk were sprinkled with sodden pieces of paper, and the person under the umbrella was walking rapidly away.

***

WORKING GIRL

In the wee hours, but not quite dawn,
I walk up to the 24-hour grocery for a fat
Sunday Times, passing a tousled-headed blonde
Who's probably hoping for one last trick
As she waits for the BART to open.
She's unpainted, almost waif-like.

I imagine a tiny place in the East Bay, maybe
A part-time weekday job, and two small children
Home asleep, entwined in each other's arms.
There's rent to pay, utilities, and because
There's no one else, she must remember to
Stop at the corner bodega for groceries.

Back home, I note the window across the street.

He has company: a tousled-headed blonde.
She stands under the bright overhead
In bra and panties while he lazes against
The pillows, waving his arms, orchestrating.
A budding film director who wrote the script.
She walks to the window and closes the curtains.

***

SLUMMING

Around the corner on O'Farrell Street,
We order a table dance at Mitchell Brothers.
For extra, we get a pair and a choice of toy.
The action site's groomed, lightly scented, and
Placed smack in the middle of the small table.
When we tell them we want their favorite toy,
They choose a silver, Montblanc-sized vibrator
That sounds like someone softly humming.
"Sold at the gift shop," the one says, as she
Strokes it repeatedly against the other's flower.
We witness an unmistakable shudder,
As if water's been turned to wine,
Or loaves and fishes multiplied,
Or your mouth's upon my pussy.
It was not a shudder that could be faked.

***

LUNCH WITH FRANCIS

It was a Chinese place, a hole in the wall on Kearney Street, and it was packed.

The girl said, "You know who comes here, don't you?"

"I know who you mean," the woman answered. "Aren't we right near his office?"

"Yeah, and this place won't let autograph seekers in to bother him.

I'm really hungry," the woman said.

The pair had walked up through Chinatown and into North Beach. Before that they had been window-shopping the streets and alleys east of

Union Square when something had caught girl's eye.

"Look at that color," the girl said. "I love that color!"

The jacket could only be described as ... Eggplant, with a capital E. Not purple, but a deep, luscious shade of ... Eggplant. They went in and the girl asked to see the item in the window.

"You will never guess who was just here," the salesperson said, handing the jacket to the girl. "Sally Fields!"

"Was she nice?" the woman asked.

"Ohmygod, I'm still shaking all over," the salesperson said, and held up her hands to prove it.

The girl, wearing the beautiful jacket, was admiring herself in the large mirror. The woman reached over and flipped the dangling tag to read the price.

"Beautiful," she said to the girl, "but we need to keep moving."

"Oh, mom, I love it," the girl exclaimed. But she eased it off her shoulders and handed it back to the salesperson. The pair then window-shopped all the way up Grant, and through Chinatown.

In a North Beach Chinese hole in wall they were

taken to the very last table, next to the kitchen door. The girl, with her back to the next table, squeezed herself in between the two and settled herself on the banquette. The woman took the chair facing but wondered how the large man sitting beside her daughter could ever have squeezed himself through that tiny gap. He was with three other people.

The girl ordered for them, and when the woman handed the menus back to the waitress she asked for a beer. With a glass, she added.

When the beer and the glass arrived, the woman poured and then handed the glass to the girl. They clicked, glass to bottle. "To ...," the woman said, then shrugged and didn't know what to say. Suddenly she had suddenly recognized the burly bearded man seated diagonally across. The woman felt her face warming and took a large swallow of beer, hoping it would bring the color down.

When their food arrived, the girl divided it between their two plates. As she did so, the large man leaned over, sniffing with appreciation. "Good choice," he said, and pointed out that the place was careful to slice the sweet potatoes thickly, so they didn't fall apart.

The girl glanced at the man seated beside her.

Quickly, she turned back to face her mother, and opened her eyes as wide as they would go, mimicking total shock.

The woman managed to choke back her laughter. "Such a beautiful color," she said to the man, "although I am not usually fond of the color orange."

"All colors need a compliment," the large man said, "you will find that dish is exquisite, for such an otherwise ordinary...," he paused and twirled his fork in the air, indicating where they were. "Next time," he added, "try it with the eggplant."

The woman smiled and wondered how she was supposed to eat and converse normally with her daughter when seated across from that particular person. She noticed he rarely spoke to the other three people at his table, but he continued to watch and comment on their progress through the meal. At one point, he complimented their good appetites. When he and his party left, with tables shifted quite a bit to ease his exit, the woman signaled the waitress and ordered another beer.

"He was flirting with you," the girl said.

"He was not," the woman answered.

"You look like his wife," the girl said. "How she

looked back when she filmed the movie about the movie."

The woman shrugged. "Could be," she said.

Over their second shared beer they discussed the few things they still needed to buy. They were leaving town, bugging out as her military father would say. The woman was tired of the city and wanted to live again with the color green.

When they left, she noted the coppery-green of the stately building at the corner of Kearney and Columbus. The style was so old she wondered if it was a survivor of the '06 'quake. The woman tilted her chin toward the building.

"Yeah," the girl said, "he owns the whole thing."

"Come," the woman said. "Let's go back and get that jacket."

***

MEXICO

THE TOURIST

Gabriel has made himself at ease on the matrimonial bed, ankles crossed, head cushioned by the mountain of white-cased pillows piled against the headboard. There's an open suitcase at the foot of the bed, and an open bottle of Chilean red on the bedside table. He takes careful sips from the glass in hand, as he watches his sister-in-law move about the room.

Taking a suit from the closet, Carolina puts it to her nose and sniffs. She detects a definite odor of cigarettes, yet she knows Gabriel doesn't smoke. She wonders if maybe he sneaks and smokes when he goes off on trips.

"No suits," he tells her when he sees what she's holding. Says he's thinking of wearing jeans and a leather jacket, something to show he can't be pushed around, something that can handle a little blood when he punches somebody in the nose.

Carolina laughs, she knows he's making a joke. He won't be punching anyone at his business meetings. "Take the suit," she says, "and you can wear jeans on the plane."

He makes his mouth small and narrows his eyes, as if he's considering, but it's all part of the game. He teases her and she loves the attention.

Draping the suit over the back of a chair, she goes to the dresser. From a drawer she takes two starched and folded shirts. After placing them in the suitcase, she tells him she thinks he might need a sweater. She reminds him the evenings can be cool.

The bedroom door swings open wide with a thump and two small faces peer into the room: Marco and Marie Claire, bathed and ready for bed. When they see the suitcase, they look wide-eyed from Carolina to their father.

"Remember," Carolina says to them, "the Owl?"

"Oh! The owl," they shout, and stampede into the room. Hooting and hopping, they prance up and across the bed and over their father's legs while the suitcase bounces merrily.

Gabriel holds high his glass of wine, so it doesn't spill all over his wife's pristine white bedcover.

"Manuela!" He yells for the housekeeper.

"Come get these kids!" Manuela has already changed from her uniform to a pink bathrobe.

"*Gracias, gracias,*" Gabriel says to her, and he takes good-night kisses from the children. "Now, your auntie," he reminds them, and they give Carolina kisses, too.

Before they leave, Gabriel wags his finger and tells them: "Remember, it's the red-eye, not the owl."

They turn to him. "Huh?"

"In English," he says, "it's not the owl, it's the red-eye."

The red-eye, Carolina silently tells herself. But she knows that whatever the name, English or Spanish, it's the late-night flight that will take Gabriel from Houston to Mexico City, to his important meetings to which he will wear the suit she has chosen for him.

"What's going on?" Elena frowns at them both from the doorway. To her sister she asks: "Why are you doing this?" She crosses the room, removes her earrings and plinks them into a china dish on the dresser. She turns to her husband. "You need to do your own packing," she tells him as she kicks off her shoes.

"But I don't mind," Carolina says. "It's fun to help."

"Fun," Gabriel repeats. "We're having fun."

"You're incorrigible," Elena says to him.

"Incorrigible," he mimics, then turns to his sister-in-law. "Am I, Caro?"

Carolina shrugs and says nothing. She doesn't know what the word means.

Elena goes into the adjoining bathroom but leans back out the doorway and says to Gabriel: "You remind me of that Garcia-Marquez story."

He groans and holds up a hand, like a traffic cop, telling her to stop. "Don't give me Gabo," he says. "Spare me."

She tells him anyway: "You're exactly like that drunk traveling salesman who is dancing with two women at the same time. Yes, he's sooooo drunk and sooooo happy. He could not be any happier if besides his arms and his legs, he also had a tail." Elena turns and shuts the bathroom door.

"A tail?" Gabriel shouts, then turning to Carolina he rolls his eyes.

"Why do you say Gabo's name so meanly?" Carolina asks, "you don't like him, do you think he's bad?"

"No, not at all, I'm in awe of him. He has a vivid imagination and is dreamy just like you, Caro, only he writes it down and gets paid a lot of money."

"Does that make him bad?"

"No, Caro, to me, he is a holy man and being

dreamy is a gift. Now my ties, Caro. We know how important it is to select the correct ties."

Carolina laughs. Choosing ties is her favorite part of helping him pack. Already she is missing him. After he's gone there will be only Elena constantly telling her about her messy hair, that she dresses like a peasant and walks like a clodhopper -- whatever that is. Over and over Elena tells her: A little make-up wouldn't hurt. Don't you want to look better? To that, Carolina always answers that the way she looks is just fine with her.

There are also red-eye buses, or the owl, as Carolina still prefers, and the next day she packs a small valise. She takes her time to carefully write a note saying she is going home to Mama's. That evening, when the household has gone to bed, she puts the note in the kitchen where Manuela will find it in the morning and calls a taxi. At the bus station she buys a ticket from Houston to San Luis Potosi.

The next afternoon the bus stops at a small town and everyone gets out to stretch, and maybe get a quick bite of something. Across the square Carolina notices a small bus bound for the nearby mountain village *Real de Catorce*. It's idling, waiting for more passengers. Quickly she buys a ticket and runs toward it. The driver sees her and holds the door.

The bus chugs out of town. Her fellow passengers are three men who seem to be sleeping off hangovers and a woman with a bundle of *serapes* and embroidered blouses. The narrow ancient road, paved with cobblestones, winds up the mountain. To avoid looking down on the sheer drop of hundreds of feet to the valley floor, Carolina sits on the mountain side of the bus.

When they reach the centuries-old tunnel that passes through the mountain, the driver stops and cuts the motor. Carolina moves to the other side of the bus where she can watch for the man with the walkie-talkie at the entrance. The tunnel is only wide enough for one-way traffic. The bus waits. A Volkswagen so old it no longer has a color pulls up behind, and behind that a Coca-Cola truck. The sleeping men still sleep, the woman with her wares says nothing, and the driver sits with his back to them all.

Finally, the man with the walkie-talkie signals and the bus driver starts the engine. Two vehicles emerge from the tunnel: a smart-looking silver car and a battered white van.

The tunnel is two kilometers long and the only illumination a single overhead bulb at the halfway mark. So, for one long kilometer and then another there is only the weight of the mountain pressing down in the darkness. Carolina feels her arms become too heavy to lift and the air seems scanty. She tries to empty her mind of fear. She takes small breaths and practices dying.

When the bus emerges from the tunnel, into the dazzling daylight, it stops in a wide empty parking area. With the others, Carolina staggers off. She feels as unsteady on her feet as the men with hangovers. She follows the slow-moving Coca-Cola truck as it rumbles along, bottles knocking against each other, into the village.

At the stalls lining the market street she sees few customers, although the air smells deliciously of roasted goat. She turns into a steep narrow side street, and passes a café named The Black Cat. One of the outside tables is occupied by a young foreign couple with long tanned legs and hiking boots. A little farther on is the small plaza, where a woman wearing a sky-blue apron is raking the flower beds.

Continuing to trudge slowly uphill, Carolina finally reaches the whitewashed hotel on the far edge of the village. It seems the same, although she notices the balustrades along the upper walkways are now painted a gaudy red and adorned with *Café Bustelo* cans blooming with red geraniums. As before, the hotel is a work in progress with spikes of rebar jutting from the roof. A statue of Saint Francis stands in the upper garden. When she looks down into the lower garden, she sees the large concrete Buddha has now been painted that same gaudy red.

The proprietor remembers Carolina from the time before and asks for the health of her sister and the children.

"Fine," she tells him, "they are all fine."

The time before: Elena had driven down with the children from Houston to Potosi to visit Mama. Carolina had been listening at the door when Mama told Elena: "She is so stubborn. Please, see if you can do something, anything with her."

Carolina had been happy to be leaving and going to live with Elena in Houston. She was tired of Mama's complaints that she spent too much time in the kitchen with the maids instead of working on finding herself a husband. Although Carolina had always been fond of both her own father and Elena's Gabriel, she had never truly understood the benefit of having a husband.

On the long drive from Potosi to Houston, Elena decided they would take what she said would be an amusing side trip, up to a small mountain village, a place that is called 'Pueblo Mágico' she had read about in a guidebook.

They settled into the hotel, then visited the two churches. The one near the hotel was a ruin with pigeons nesting on the inside ledge of a partially collapsed Moorish-style dome. The other church, in the central plaza, had a floor of wooden coffin tops that shifted and creaked, making spooky sounds with every step.

Carolina had noticed an older man sitting in the sun outside that church. His face was as waxy and pale as the statues inside. He was wearing a hat such as fishermen wear, and he was reading from a small, leather-covered book. The hotel proprietor had told them to look for such a man as he had the keys to the *palenque*. Just ask, they were told, and he will show it to you.

The man with the fisherman's hat reminded Carolina of the tall German who lived next door at Mama's who also had a very long, pale face. Every day when Carolina and the maids slipped out for a cigarette before lunch, they would watch him from Mama's dining room balcony. He would yell to the boys who worked for him, demanding the keys. "The keys, the keys, give me the keys, *dame las llaves!*" he shouted. His courtyard was full of fancy cars. How did the boys know which keys he meant?

Elena had not been interested in seeing the *palenque*. "It's just some dusty arena," she said. "They probably use it for cock fights." Instead they went to an old building that had once been the mint. It had been divided into artisan stalls and Elena shopped for earrings. She bought a pair of small silver balls for Marie Claire and a pair of large silver hoops for herself. She scolded Carolina for refusing every pair she insisted were perfect for her.

Meanwhile the children had become cranky with hunger. Elena found a restaurant on a nearby side street. The menu posted in the window listed spaghetti, lasagna, and other Italian dishes. Although the sign said open, the door was locked. When Elena knocked and then rattled it, a sleepy sounding voice called down from a small balcony, a girl who said they were open.

"But the door is locked," Elena called back, her neck stretched long like a goose.

They waited and finally the door opened. Carolina could see that the girl's cheek had been marked by a crease in her siesta pillow. They followed her past a dark dining room, and into an inner courtyard where there was light and where steps led up to a second-floor gallery. "We have lasagna," the girl said.

Elena answered that the children would prefer plain pasta with butter. The girl frowned and repeated that there was lasagna. Meanwhile Marco scooted up the steps toward the second floor.

Elena called him back and sent him to sit in the darkened dining room. "Surely," Elena said to the girl, "plain pasta could not be a problem, perhaps with some cheese and a few sautéed mushrooms."

Then Marie Claire started up the steps. Elena grabbed her by the arm and marched her over to stand against the wall. Such a pitiful little figure, Carolina thought, with her forehead pressed to the dusty wall, her tiny shoulders shaking theatrically in silent sobs. Truth was, Carolina thought Marco and Marie Claire were charming only when then they were in distress. Otherwise, under her breath, she called them brats.

The girl then explained that the power was off, but that the lasagna had been left in the oven and might still be warm enough to serve.

"Never mind," Elena said, throwing her arms in the air.

They all returned to the hotel where they were told the power was off in the whole village. So, they sat on the terrace and drank warmish beers and cokes and ate cold tamales. After that they watched the children toss bottle caps in the fountain and terrorize Michael, the hotel dog. That was all. Early the next morning they left for Houston.

The hotel registration card asks for occupation. Officially, Carolina thinks, I am the Sister of the Family, or the Auntie, or the Daughter. Now, at last, she tells herself she is none of those. She writes Tourist.

When she asks where she might find the man with the keys to the *palenque*, she's told to look for him in one plaza or the other. Then, although she protests, the proprietor insists on carrying her small valise up to the room. Jose, the fellow who usually carries the bags, he explains, is occupied repairing the stonework around the fountain.

"Soon," he says, "we will be very busy."

"Soon," Carolina asks?

"In October," he says, "when the pilgrims come for the feast of Saint Francis. They come for the miracles."

"Are there miracles," she asks?

He shrugs. Laughs.

"Are there?" Carolina repeats.

"Who knows," he says, unlocking the door to the same room they had before.

Nothing has changed. The same thread-bare bedspreads and rough blankets, the same flat pillows, and the door to the bathroom still just a plastic curtain. Carolina kicks off her shoes, rinses her feet in the shower. In the mottled mirror she decides she looks like her grandmother.

When she glances out the small window, down to the vast desert disappearing into the horizon, she can see eternity.

In the far corner of the hotel dining room Carolina sees the young foreign couple she had noticed earlier at the cafe in the village. They are too far away for her to hear what language they are speaking. She envies their fine hiking boots. Stretching out one leg, she turns her foot like this and like that and imagines a fine hiking-boot instead of her shoe, the one especially fitted with a lift for her short leg.

When the proprietor's wife brings her plate of *cabrito*, beans, and *ensalada*, Carolina changes chairs and sits with her back to the couple. To her left is a window looking out over the desert and the distant mountain ranges. Through the windows on her right, she can see the hotel's collection of bird cages hanging beneath the eaves. The occupants of the cages, mostly parakeets, are oddly silent. Carolina thinks they look sickly.

After eating, she decides to walk back into the village. But soon she begins to feel weak. Perhaps it's the altitude, she thinks. She stops to rest on a low wall.

Between the wall and the cliff's steep drop sits a small house, and in the courtyard a vehicle that looks like a Jeep. The door to the house opens and out steps a young woman in a bathrobe of white toweling. Her hair is pale and fluffy. Like an angel, Carolina thinks.

"Fuck you," the young woman who looks like an angel shouts back through the doorway.

Surprised by the 'angel's' vulgarity, Carolina stands abruptly and ambles away toward the village, to the small plaza. The place is empty, and she finds a place to sit.

In the shade of the tall trees the air smells of damp earth and damask. The rose bushes surrounding the bandstand are huge old shrubs. She hears only faint sounds drifting up from the market street below.

Carolina knows the man with the keys will be in one plaza or the other. She watches and knows he will be carrying that leather-covered book, which may be a missal or a bible. Although the hotel proprietor's wife, when Carolina asked, assured her the man was not a priest.

As Carolina waits, she anticipates. She knows the man is a holy man just like Garcia-Marquez, and soon he will sit down on the bench across from her and ask if she wants to visit the *palenque*.

"Not yet," she will answer. "Could we just sit for

a while?"

"For as long as you wish."

"Forever?"

"If you wish."

And while she waits, the plaza fills with the ghosts of young men in stiff collars and young women in taffeta skirts, courting in an endless paseo. The sound of wind in the tall trees mimics the swish of the women's skirts, as around and around they whirl, while black-clad *duennas* look on.

Carolina hears the snip, snip of scissors. The woman she saw earlier raking the beds is now removing the faded blooms and collecting the scented petals in the pockets of her sky-blue apron. And she hears the voice of the tall German shouting *Dame las llaves*! As he did every day at eleven o'clock at Mama's house when she and the maids would sneak out onto the balcony for forbidden cigarettes.

Everyone wants keys, she thinks, and here, the old holy man in the fisherman's hat has keys. All Carolina has to do is wait. She knows that someday he will give her those keys.

***

EL GUAPO

We were in Merida and Solange said, "You *must* meet him. He's *gorgeous.*"

She fluttered her hands like she does and sat down beneath the Modigliani and assumed the same pose.

As she kept waving her hands, her fingers grew longer and when she tucked up her legs to hide her thick ankles, she looked just like the picture.

As I sat watching her transformation, a man came into the room. His face was flat like an ancient Olmec carving.

"Isn't he *gorgeous?*" Solange said.

"Perhaps to an anthropologist," I answered.

"But that's what I am," she cried.

The man shifted the gun belts across his shoulders and said nothing.

***

LOUISIANA

ICE STORM, MANSFIELD

A translucent layer of silver coats every tree limb,
Every pine needle and blade of grass.
Power's out. To warm the house the oven
Door's propped open and on top something
Stew-like set to simmer.

Wearing sweats and sweaters and heavy socks,
Hands wrapped around a mug of hot chocolate,
I read Fawn Brodie's Jefferson by window-light,
Knowing he had purchased the land outside
At Napoleon's fire sale.

If deer season's over, why these spooky sounds
Of gunfire? Perhaps hallucinary echoes
Of a Civil War battle fought nearby?

No. It's merely the snap of tree branches
Burdened by their silvery weight.

Toward dusk I venture out, into the icy Nordic
Fairyland to find the driveway's now impassible,
Barricaded by a long row of broken pine saplings
Whose raw flesh perfumes the air with the startling
Scent of oranges.

***

MY FATHER'S WATCH

A rural place in the deep south, a basic cabin needing renovation, a good-sized pond and land for a garden. For this I gladly traded a busy city's concrete landscape of dull browns and greys, city canyons formed by tall buildings allowing only a sliver of sky. I was starved for the color green.

The long, narrow driveway opened onto seven acres bounded by pine trees. A large pond, rimmed in sedges, hosted water snakes, and red-eared sliders who sunned themselves on fallen logs. Occasionally fish jumped, and great blue herons and snowy egrets could be seen high stepping in the shallows.

The lawn mower was sluggish, a gas-fueled, antique walk-behind. Six days of walking and thinking, then one day of rest, and begin again. As the season slipped toward deep summer, I stripped to underwear, feet in flip-flops, hair off my neck in short braids, sometimes a straw hat. You've become as dark as an Indian, my father said.

I learned about fire ants, sumac, poison ivy, castor beans, and to admire the flowers and huge leaves of the catalpa. I learned to use an oar and not my hand as a lever to flip the overturned rowboat as moccasins loved to nap in the shade. At night I listened to the hoof beats of a visiting family of deer.

The pond had three year-round feathered residents: a delicate female mallard and two generic white ducks who spent all their waking hours chasing her to fuck, fuck, fuck. My father shook his head, and I shook mine, but we both understood: those dumb ducks were only doing what nature told them to.

The place also came with a part Shepard mutt, female, a thief who stole rags, gloves, and my father's underwear. We'd find these items buried in shallow graves around the yard. She was a trash dog, unwelcome everywhere for that nasty habit. One day she never returned, and we figured someone shot her.

That first summer my father built a greenhouse

from a kit. It leaned against the south side of the cabin. He tiled the floor and opened it into the bedrooms with sliding glass doors. He also dreamed of cutting down a copse to open space for a lighter than air to lift off and land. Flying was his life.

In the VA hospital in Shreveport the orderlies turned a blind eye to the small granddaughter slipping into the room. Almost all of us were there, a rather carnival atmosphere. I held his hand. His face was gaunt. He looked so much like me. Is that all? he asked. Yes, I said. He nodded and closed his eyes.

Early the next morning the hospital called. He was gone. Yet, for months I could hear the chimes of his wristwatch set to remind him to stay busy, as if he ever needed reminding of that. What I heard was not an hallucination nor a dreamy-dream, but a mockingbird who had learned the music of my father's watch.

***

ABOUT THE AUTHOR

Mitchell Hagerstrom, the author of this collection, began writing in college in the 1970s. She was raised in a peripatetic military family and continued that vagabond sort of life throughout the 70s, 80s, and 90s.

The locales of the pieces in this collection more or less follow her wanderings: Southern California, Missouri, San Francisco, Louisiana, and a jaunt into Mexico. Five years of the 80s were spent in Micronesia which became the setting for her first two books, *Miss Gone-overseas* and *Overseas Stories*. For the past twenty years she has lived in Austin, Texas.

For more information visit Mitchell at her Miss Gone Overseas pages on Facebook, Goodreads and Amazon Author's Central.

OTHER WORKS BY MITCHELL HAGERSTROM

"MISS GONE OVERSEAS", (Karayuki-san), Pillow Book published 2012 by Tiny Toe Press, New version 2nd Edition paperback and e-Book published by Penryn Editions 2019

"OVERSEAS STORIES", sequel to Miss Gone Overseas, e-Book version published 2012 by Tiny Toe Press, 2nd Edition paperback and e-book published 2019 by Penryn Editions.